D1335469

SCREAM STREET

TERROR OF THE NIGHTWATCHMAN

"Genuinely funny and genuinely sp-sp-spooky,
Tommy Donbavand's Scream Street puts humorous
horror firmly on the map!"
Philip Ardagh

The fiendish fun continues at
www.screamstreet.co.uk

Other Scream Street titles

SCREAM STREET

TERROR OF THE NIGHTWATCHMAN

TOMMY DONBAVAND

**WALKER
BOOKS**

First published 2010 by Walker Books Ltd
87 Vauxhall Walk, London SE11 5HJ

4 6 8 10 9 7 5

Text © 2010 Tommy Donbavand
Illustrations © 2010 Cartoon Saloon Ltd

The right of Tommy Donbavand to be identified
as author of this work has been asserted by him in accordance
with the Copyright, Designs and Patents Act 1988

This book has been typeset in Bembo Educational

Printed and bound in Great Britain by Clays Ltd, St Ives plc

British Library Cataloguing in Publication Data: a catalogue record
for this book is available from the British Library

ISBN 978-1-4063-1914-9

www.walker.co.uk

For Aoife Donbavand,
magical and enchanting

Meet the residents...

Luke Watson

Cleo Farr

Resus Negative

Dixon

Sir Otto Sneer

Samuel Skipstone

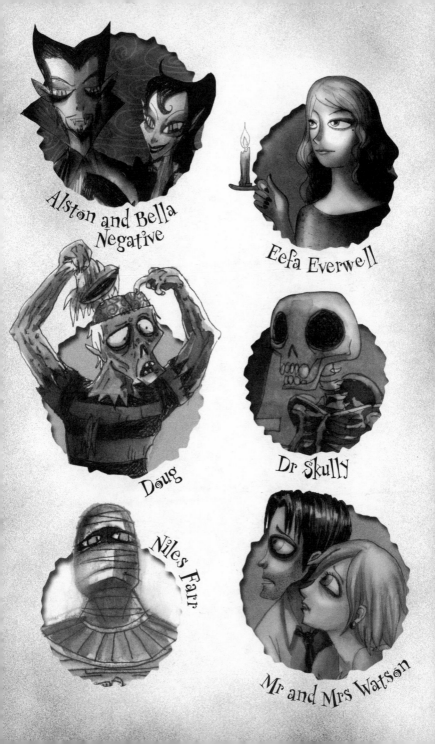

Alston and Bella Negative

Eefa Everwell

Doug

Dr Skully

Niles Farr

Mr and Mrs Watson

Who lives where...

Previously on Scream Street...

Mr and Mrs Watson were terrified when their son, Luke, first transformed into a werewolf. But that was nothing compared to their terror at being forcibly moved to Scream Street – and discovering there was no going back.

Determined to take his parents home, Luke enlisted the help of his new friends, Resus Negative, a wannabe vampire, and Cleo Farr, an Egyptian mummy, to find six relics left behind by the community's founding fathers. Only by collecting these magical artefacts would he be able to open a doorway back to his own world.

Just as Luke and his friends finally succeeded in their quest, Mr and Mrs Watson realized how happy Luke had become in his new home and decided to stay on in Scream Street. But the newly opened doorway was becoming a problem – Sir Otto Sneer, the street's wicked landlord, was charging "normals" from Luke's world to visit what he called "the world's greatest freak show".

To protect Scream Street, Luke must try to close the doorway by returning the relics to their original owners – although he and Resus will have to embark on a terrifying rescue mission first...

Chapter One
The Awakening

The vampire ran as fast as he could. He could see the house up ahead, dawn sunlight shimmering off the roof tiles. Gritting his teeth, he leapt into the air and twirled his cape. In a burst of black smoke, the vampire changed into a small bat.

The bat pumped its wings and sped on, screeching, catching the high-pitched echoes with its sensitive ears and using them to navigate the dead trees that lined the road.

When it reached the house, the bat perched on a branch that overlooked a bedroom window. Although it was blind in this form, the creature knew that inside a boy lay asleep, blood pumping through his veins. The bat licked its tiny fangs and launched itself from the tree … straight into the window.

Smack!

With a screech, the bat bounced off the window pane and in another cloud of smoke involuntarily transformed back into a vampire. Stretching up, he just managed to grasp the brick-work under the window. Then he hung there by his fingertips, not daring to look down.

Luke Watson jumped out of bed at the noise. He'd been dreaming he was at some kind of bizarre circus, complete with tap-dancing crows. His friends, Resus and Cleo, had been performing too, their hilarious antics causing tears of laughter to pour down his face—

"Help!"

Luke dashed to the window. He slid it up and peered out. "Hello?"

"Hello!" answered a voice.

Luke looked down to see a familiar figure grinning up at him. "Kian!" he exclaimed. "What are you doing there?"

"I'm a vampire!" declared his young neighbour.

Luke grabbed Kian by his wrists and dragged him into the bedroom. "I know you're a vampire – but they don't usually throw themselves at first-floor windows."

"I didn't throw myself at it," protested Kian, brushing brick dust from his cloak. "I was a bat. I flew into it."

"I thought bats had that sonar thing to stop them doing that?"

Kian nodded. "They do, but I'm not very good at it yet."

"It's not a problem," smiled Luke. "I like waking up to the soothing sound of something slamming against a pane of glass." He picked up his watch from his bedside table and peered at it. "Kian – it's four-thirty in the morning! What's going on?"

"Resus sent me to get you as soon as I could," explained the vampire. "There's a problem."

Luke yawned. "What kind of problem can't wait until a more reasonable hour of the day?"

"Cleo is missing."

Luke raced across Scream Street's central square, pulling on a T-shirt. Kian followed. Cleo's house was in one of the roads on the far side of the square and Luke skidded to a halt as he reached the garden gate. He saw that the front door had been smashed in.

Dashing inside, Luke found the house beginning to fill with residents. Cleo's father, Niles Farr, was deep in conversation with Resus. Luke

 14

hurried over. "Thank you for coming," said the giant mummy.

"No problem," Luke assured him. "My mum and dad are just getting dressed; they'll be here soon. What happened?"

"I do not know," explained Niles. "I woke to hear a smash, and when I went to investigate, Cleo was no longer in her sarcophagus."

"The smash must have been the front door," said Luke.

"Or the door to Cleo's room," added Resus. "That's been kicked in too."

"You didn't see anything?" Luke asked Niles.

"As I ran down the stairs I thought I saw movement," replied the mummy solemnly. "But it was only shadows."

"It must have been the normals!" cried a phantom. "They've taken her!"

"There's been nothing but trouble since that doorway was opened," added a gargoyle. Several residents turned to fix Luke with accusing stares.

"We don't know *who* took Cleo," said Dr Skully, the children's skeletal teacher. "And until we do, let's keep an open mind. Now, I shall

team up with Twinkle to search house numbers 1–10 for any sign of her."

As the skeleton continued, Scream Street's three resident zombies arrived. "Bella will assist Doug and Berry in searching 11–20; Eefa, Turf and Alston will take 21–30; and 31–40 will be handled by the Crudleys and the Watsons."

"Who's searching Sneer Hall?" enquired Alston Negative.

"I've sent the Movers there to rouse Sir Otto," Dr Skully replied. "That way, we have the whole street covered."

"Who should Resus and I go with?" Luke asked.

The skeleton frowned at him. "You two are going straight back to bed," he ordered. "Kian too. We don't want any more missing children tonight."

"But Cleo's our friend!" protested Luke.

"And the grown-ups will find her," said the teacher firmly.

"I'll stay here with Niles," offered Tibia Skully. "I think he could do with a nice cup of lotus-flower tea."

"That would be very kind of you, my dear,"

said Dr Skully, smiling at his wife. He turned back to the others. "And, finally, if anyone finds the girl they should immediately send word to Miss Everwell."

The witch nodded. "I've got a spell ready that will light a beacon on the roof of the emporium as soon as we know she's safe."

"And if no light appears?" asked Alston.

"We meet back here in two hours," said Dr Skully. "Now, let's get out there and find Cleo."

The room quickly emptied as the residents set off to search.

Luke turned and headed for the stairs. "Come on," he hissed to Resus.

"Where are you going?" asked the vampire.

"Cleo's room," replied Luke.

"But Dr Skully told us to go back to bed."

"And you're going to listen to him? We might find some clues up there to tell us who's taken her."

"So you think she's been kidnapped?" said Resus.

Luke shrugged. "Cleo can be strong-minded sometimes, but it's not like her to disappear of her own accord."

The boys crept up the stairs and climbed over the splintered remains of the bedroom door. "That's made from Transylvanian oak," said Resus. "Just about the strongest wood there is. It will have taken something with a fair few muscles to smash up a door like that."

They began to search the room. "Doesn't it strike you as odd that Cleo's dad was woken up by a crash, but by the time he'd crossed the landing from his room, Cleo – and whoever had taken her – had gone?" said Luke.

"No more odd than Cleo going quietly," grinned Resus.

"So, whoever took Cleo was fast *and* had a way to keep her quiet," said Luke thoughtfully, sitting on the golden sarcophagus that the young mummy used as a bed.

"But why smash the doors?" asked Resus. "I can understand they'd have to break in downstairs, but I doubt the bedroom door was locked."

Luke knelt down beside the broken door and began to rummage through the debris. "Maybe something here will tell us," he said. He picked up the golden doorknob and gave a yelp before dropping it again and rubbing his hands furiously on his jeans.

"What's the matter?" asked Resus. "Is it hot? Cold?"

Luke shook his head. "No, it's... I don't know. As soon as I touched it, I felt as though I was going to cry!"

"Cry?" scoffed Resus. "How can a doorknob make you cry?" He snatched up the handle and held it for a moment before hurling it across the room with a shudder. "What's *wrong* with that thing?" he demanded.

"I'm not sure it's the doorknob itself," said

Luke. "It felt as if there was some kind of slimy stuff on it – although I can't see anything on my hands."

"This is getting weirder!" exclaimed Resus, looking down at his own hands. "First Cleo goes missing, and now we've got a doorknob that makes you depressed."

"There must be something else here to help us," sighed Luke in frustration.

Resus shrugged. "Smashed door, sad handle… I can't see anything else."

Luke looked thoughtful. "Then maybe we're just not looking at it in the right way…" Sitting back on his heels, he concentrated on feeling angry over Cleo's disappearance.

Since he had arrived in Scream Street, Luke had learned how to trigger his werewolf transformations, and had developed the ability to transform just one part of his body at a time. Now he focused the anger on the upper part of his face. Slowly, his eyes began to change from their usual brown to a bright, vivid yellow and his nose stretched to form a snout.

Once the partial transformation was complete, Luke turned back to the broken door and looked

down at it through his werewolf eyes. He gasped.

"What is it?" asked Resus. "What can you see?"

"The door handle's covered in some sort of green goo!" Luke exclaimed. "That must be what made us feel sad when we touched it!" He stared at the emerald substance he could now also see smeared over his hands and splashed across Cleo's bedroom walls and furniture. "But something bothers me about the smell…"

Resus sniffed at the air. "I can't smell anything," he said, "but then I haven't got your werewolf nostrils."

Luke swallowed hard. "I can taste copper at the back of my throat," he said, his snout twitching. "This stuff smells like blood."

Chapter Two
The Rip

It was almost light by the time the boys emerged from Cleo's house.

"What kind of creature has invisible sadness blood?" asked the vampire as they began to follow the trail of emerald goo down the street and into the central square.

"I've no idea," admitted Luke, "but if it's bleeding, that probably means Cleo fought back and hurt it."

Resus smiled despite himself. "That sounds more like her!"

"Look – the trail heads right past the doorway," said Luke. The boys glanced over at the rainbow-coloured portal to Luke's old world, which they had opened by collecting together six relics left behind by Scream Street's founding fathers.

"We'd better keep a low profile," suggested Resus. "Dr Skully thinks we've gone back to bed. He won't be too happy if he spots us out here."

"Everyone's out searching for Cleo," said Luke. "No one will see us—"

"Except me," growled a deep voice. A hand gripped Luke by the hair and jerked his head back. Scream Street's landlord, Sir Otto Sneer, was glaring down at him, a pungent cigar clamped between his teeth. "Oh my, Grandma," he snarled. "What big eyes you've got!"

Luke pulled away. "Isn't it a bit early for you to be out of your pit?"

"Dixon and a family of extremely noisy

23

banshees are searching my mansion for your mummy friend," snarled the landlord. "So I took the opportunity to welcome today's curious normals into Scream Street myself…"

"Welcome their money into your pockets, more like," muttered Resus.

"What do you want, Sneer?" said Luke.

"You know exactly what I want," rumbled Sir Otto. "Give me the remaining relics before you get it into your freakish head to return any more of them!"

Luke stared angrily at the landlord through his werewolf eyes. Sir Otto had pounced upon the open doorway as a money-making opportunity, charging outsiders to visit what he called "the world's greatest freak show".

Luke, Resus and Cleo had decided to return the relics to their original donors in the hope that this would close the doorway and put a stop to the tide of normals touring the street. Giving back the first relic – a vampire's fang – had already caused the doorway to shrink a little. Sir Otto was beginning to realize that the children were intent on spoiling his lucrative scheme.

"You can't stop us," snapped Luke. "We'll

close the doorway and stop you making everyone's lives a misery!"

"Yeah," agreed Resus. "We're going to give back the bottle of witch's blood just as soon as we find Cleo."

Luke sighed. In one breath, Resus had given away the identity of the relic they planned to return next *and* the fact that they were on Cleo's trail!

Sir Otto's face split into a wide grin. "So, it's the bottle of blood next?" he beamed, blowing cigar smoke over the boys. "That's very interesting to hear…" The smile quickly vanished. "Hand it over!"

Luke glared at the landlord, bathed yellow in his werewolf vision. "Unless you want to see some big teeth to match these big eyes, I'd leave us alone."

Sir Otto flushed, but he decided against pressing the matter further. "I'll be watching you!" he growled before spinning on his heels and stomping back towards his stool.

"You don't think Sneer himself took Cleo, do you?" said Resus. "You know – to try to stop us giving back any more relics."

Luke shook his head. "He couldn't risk her being found by one of the adults," he said. "He's just trying to wind us up. Come on…"

They followed the blood around the side of Everwell's Emporium to a spot near the stock-room door, where the trail abruptly ended. "That's it," said Luke, his eyes shrinking as they returned to normal. "No more blood."

"What now?" asked Resus, looking around. "They can't have just vanished!"

Luke sighed. "I've no idea," he admitted.

"Right," said Resus, "let's think… We know that whatever took Cleo was— *Aargh!*" With a cry of surprise, the vampire disappeared into thin air.

Luke spun round. "Resus!" he yelled. "Where are you?"

Resus's head reappeared, looking as though it was hanging in the air. "There's no need to shout!" said the vampire. "I'm only here."

Luke stared. "But where," he asked, "*is* here?" He reached out towards the space below Resus's neck. There was a rip in the air, as though someone had cut a slit into a curtain in front of him.

"It's a Hex Hatch!" he breathed.

Resus examined the rip. The Hex Hatches they had encountered in the past had all been tidy, square openings that led from one G.H.O.U.L. community to another. This was similar, yet different. "I thought only Trackers could open Hex Hatches," he said.

"I doubt Zeal Chillchase had anything to do with this one," said Luke, running his fingers along the rough edge of the invisible tear.

"Where does it lead?" asked Resus.

"You're the one who just fell through," said Luke. "You tell me!" He pushed his head through the rip and found himself in another world altogether. A dense jungle stretched away from them as far as the eye could see. Hot, bright sunlight filtered down through the lush green vegetation and the cries of unfamiliar birds filled the air.

Resus rested his hand on a patch of dense undergrowth. Suddenly, he sobbed and began to rub at his palm. "The sad blood stuff!" he cried. "I've just put my hand in some more of it!"

"Then whatever it was definitely took Cleo through here," said Luke, stepping all the way through the tear and into the jungle. "We have to follow."

27

"By ourselves?" exclaimed Resus. "That thing can smash through Transylvanian oak and it bleeds pure unhappiness! I say we go back and get reinforcements."

"You saw the way Dr Skully was with us," said Luke. "He wouldn't believe us."

"OK, not Dr Skully, then," said Resus. "Your parents – or mine!"

Luke shook his head. "There isn't time," he said. "Whatever took Cleo is getting further away by the second. We have to follow its tracks now, before they start to disappear. And you know that Cleo would drop everything to set off and rescue one of us."

Resus sighed. "Why did you have to bring that up? Come on, then – before I change my mind."

Together the boys set off into the jungle. Luke transformed his eyes and nose once more so that he could see the trail, although it was now much harder to spot splashes of the creature's blood on the leaves and tree roots at their feet.

Unfamiliar sounds echoed through the jungle, and the sun, although masked by the tree canopy above, was strong enough to cause the

pair to sweat profusely.

The foliage seemed to be closing in around them, and the further they walked, the harder it became to push their way through the thick vegetation. "The kidnapper didn't leave much of a path," Luke pointed out. "Have you got anything we can use to cut through this?"

"Sure have!" Resus grinned and pulled a chainsaw from his cloak. He poised his finger over the starter button.

Luke quickly pulled the vampire's hand away. "Use that thing and we'll be heard for miles!" he hissed. "We might as well use a megaphone to announce that we're on our way to rescue Cleo!"

Reluctantly, Resus slid the chainsaw away and produced a machete instead. "You always spoil my fun," he grumbled. He began to hack at the branches, pausing every now and then to allow Luke to locate the next droplet of blood.

Eventually, they came to a stop. "This is where it ends," said Luke, allowing his features to shrink back to normal. "Whatever's got Cleo must have stopped bleeding – or else found a way to heal the wound."

"So what do we do now?"

Luke shrugged. "Beats me, but it might help to know which country we're in for a start…" He put his hand into his jeans pocket, then sighed heavily.

"What's the matter?"

"I must have left *The G.H.O.U.L. Guide* at home when I ran over to Cleo's house this morning," said Luke. "We haven't even got Mr Skipstone to help us."

"What about these?" Resus bent to collect a handful of feathers that lay at their feet. "Do they give us some kind of clue?"

"They could have been here for ages," said Luke. "This place is swarming with all kinds of exotic birds."

Resus tucked the machete back under his cape. "In that case I'm stumped," he admitted.

"We could climb a tree to see if we can spot anything from higher up," Luke suggested.

The vampire peered at the thick canopy above them. "You want to climb up there?"

"Have you got a better idea?"

"Unfortunately not," sighed Resus. He turned and stabbed his strong vampire nails into the bark of a nearby tree and began to pull himself

upwards. "But I lent all my rope to Twinkle last week, so we'll be doing this the hard way too!"

"Fair enough," said Luke, "but some of us haven't got vampire fingernails! Even my were-wolf claws wouldn't take my full bodyweight."

"No problem," beamed Resus, pulling one hand away from the tree trunk and plunging it into his pocket. He dropped ten metallic fake nails down to Luke. "Look after them – they're my spares!"

Luke slipped the nails over the ends of his fingers, sunk them into the tree and began to climb.

Chapter Three
The Catch

By the time Luke pulled himself onto the wide branch opposite Resus, he was out of breath and his arms felt like they were on fire. "Where did you learn to climb like that?" he puffed.

Resus was perched cross-legged on his branch. "Vampires are naturally good at this sort of stuff," he said. "It comes from centuries of trying to escape angry mobs with pitchforks and torches."

Luke clambered warily to his feet, clinging tightly to the tree trunk. There was a stiff breeze, and it felt as if the tree was swaying violently – although Resus didn't seem to have any problems balancing.

"Can you see anything?" Luke asked, trying not to look down. He closed his eyes and pressed his face tightly against the rough bark.

Resus swung himself up onto a higher branch. "Not a lot," he replied, "unless you mean more trees, that is." The jungle stretched as far as he could see in every direction, with no sign of civilization. Then suddenly the vampire's attention was caught by something off to the left.

"What is it?" hissed Luke. "What can you see?"

Resus frowned. "Probably nothing," he replied. "I thought I saw a tiny glow of light for a moment, but it must be my mind playing tricks on me."

"Well, *my* mind isn't playing tricks," said

 34

Luke. "It knows I'm far higher than it ever wanted me to be."

Resus skipped over to Luke's branch and grinned. "Don't tell me the wicked werewolf is afraid of heights?" he teased.

Luke swallowed hard. "I'll just feel better when my feet are back on solid gr—"

He stopped, staring at something behind his friend.

"What's the matter?" asked Resus.

"Remember I said this place must be swarming with birds?" Luke whispered. "Well, look behind you…"

Resus slowly twisted round on his branch to see a large black bird perched nearby, watching them intently. He let out a sigh of relief. "It's just a raven! You had me going there for a minute. There are ravens all over Scream Street."

"Exactly," replied Luke. "But we're not *in* Scream Street – and I don't remember learning that they like to hang out in the jungle."

"It can't be *that* unusual," said Resus. "Look, there's another one over there. And another. Maybe they followed us through the Hex Hatch."

Sure enough, there were now several of them

 35

perched in the trees around the boys, all peering intently at them with dark, beady eyes.

"This isn't good…" Luke said quietly.

"They're just birds," said Resus. "What harm can they do?"

As if on cue, the ravens took off from their various perches and launched themselves at Luke and Resus, screeching wildly. Within seconds, the pair were lost in a churning cloud of black feathers.

Luke shielded his face as powerful wings batted him and jagged claws scratched at his skin. "Resus!" he cried, but all he could see were more and more feathers descending.

The vampire had pulled his cape over his head and was trying to curl up into a ball. Ravens were pecking and tearing at the cape with their sharp beaks.

Luke knew they had to get down from the tree. If they could get to the ground, they might be able to run deeper into the jungle, where the ravens couldn't follow. He cautiously reached out with a scratched, bleeding hand and dug the fake vampire nails into the tree trunk. Moving blindly, he swung himself off his branch. "Resus, we have to— *Aargh!*"

It was a few seconds before Luke realized he was falling. The fake nails had simply slipped from his fingers and he could still see them, lodged in the bark, before they were lost from view as the

 37

ravens dived after him. A grim thought flashed across his mind as he wondered who would reach the ground first.

"LUKE!" shouted Resus.

To Luke, everything seemed to happen in slow motion. As he crashed through the smaller branches, his vision was filled by the rapidly approaching flock of birds, beaks open wide. For a brief moment, the ravens appeared to merge together to form a snarling, shadowy creature with blazing white eyes.

Luke shook his head to clear the image. He couldn't be far from the ground now; it would only be…

"Gotcha!" cried a voice as two strong arms caught him and lay him gently on the ground. Luke gazed up in astonishment as a large, round figure turned towards the looming ravens and let loose a raucous screech of his own.

"SHACKAWWW!"

The piercing scream was like nothing Luke had ever heard and seemed to come from every direction at once. The effect was instant. The birds scattered, twisting in the air to alter their course. Within seconds, they were gone.

The figure turned back to Luke and beamed down at him through rotten teeth. "You're safe now, little lamb!"

By the time Resus reached the ground, Luke was wrapped in a blanket and had an old woolly hat slipped onto his head. A huge ogre was fussing around him.

"Seriously, I'm fine!" Luke was saying, trying just as hard to free himself from the cocoon. "There's no need to mollycoddle me!"

Resus gave a relieved grin. "That hat looks good on you," he said.

The ogre spun round and beamed at the young vampire with tears in his eyes. "Another little angel!" he cried, whipping a sheet from around his waist and stumbling towards him.

Resus backed away, hands raised. "No, it's OK," he protested. "I'm fine!"

The ogre shook his head and kept coming. He was covered from head to toe in gaudy tattoos of insects, fish and animals – and he had a neat hairstyle inked onto his scalp.

"I gots my orders!" he insisted. "Any little darlings that Spider finds, he has to treats them nice and takes them to Miss Ursula." When he reached Resus, he pulled him into his thick, hairy chest, cuddling him tightly.

"What's going on?" asked Luke. "And who's Miss Ursula?"

"Don't you worry your little head, pop-pet," soothed the ogre, stroking Resus's cheek. "Spider's here to look after you now. Nothing's going to hurts you any more!"

"Nothing was hurting us to begin with," retorted Resus, pulling himself away.

"Apart from a flock of killer ravens," Luke reminded him. He turned to the ogre. "Spider… Is that your name?"

The ogre nodded solemnly.

"Thank you for catching me," said Luke, "but how did you do that thing with the birds? How did you scare them away like that?"

Spider tapped the side of his nose. "I might looks like an ordinary ogre," he beamed, "but I've gots special powers!"

"Special powers?" said Resus. "You mean, like a superhero?"

"You coulds say that," admitted Spider. "I haves the power to take on the shape and sound of any animal, anywheres in the world."

"And birds, too?" asked Luke.

Spider nodded. "I just tolds those ravens to leaves you alone – in a language they could understands. I used the power of a sabre hawk!"

 41

"Fantastic!" exclaimed Resus.

Luke suddenly felt a glimmer of hope. "We're looking for a friend," he said. "A mummy. She went missing last night. Would you be able to help us find her?"

"I don't sees why not," answered Spider, "but I needs to takes you to Miss Ursula first. The quickest way is on the back of a speeding panther."

"You can change into a panther?" gasped Resus. *"Cool!"*

Spider closed his eyes and cricked his neck from side to side. "Stands back and prepare to be amazed!" he commanded. Then he yelled, "Power of a panther!"

Chapter Four
The Camp

"This," grumbled Resus, "is embarrassing!"

Luke smiled. The boys were looking on as Spider prepared himself for the transformation. They had expected the ogre to scream out in pain as his bones splintered and muscles reformed, as with Luke's transformations – but instead he simply waved his arms around for a moment before dropping to his knees and purring.

"Er ... is that it?" Resus asked.

"I think so," Luke replied as Spider crawled over to lick his hand. "And I think he wants us to climb aboard…" Soon the boys were perched on the ogre's back as he crawled slowly – very slowly – through the undergrowth.

An hour later, Resus still hadn't emerged from his sulk. "He scared the birds away," he grunted. "I was stupid enough to believe he was a superhero!"

"Shh!" Luke hissed, glancing behind them.

"What?" asked Resus, twisting round and almost falling off Spider's back in the process.

"I thought I heard footsteps," said Luke. "But maybe not." He leant forward and spoke into Spider's ear. "Are we nearly there yet?"

"Mowwl!" rumbled the reply. Spider paused briefly to lick the back of his hand and use it to clean his face before continuing at an unsteady plod.

"Now I *know* he's taking the plasma," Resus scowled. "I bet this Miss Ursula person doesn't even exist!"

"Oh, but she does," said a soft voice. The boys jumped as a beautiful woman with short, red hair stepped out from behind a tree.

"Another rescue, Spider?" she asked the ogre.

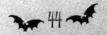

44

The ogre rose up onto his knees, causing Luke and Resus to slide off, then writhed around for a moment as though twisting himself back into human form. "Yes, Miss Ursula," he said with a wink, "and I let them into my little secret, too!"

"Little secret, my fangs!" scoffed Resus. "He hasn't got any powers at—"

Ursula gave the vampire a stern look to silence him. "Spider believes in his abilities," she said, "and as long as he's helping us, I'm willing to indulge him."

"Us?" asked Luke. "Who's us?"

Ursula smiled. "Allow me…" She clapped her hands. Instantly, dozens of children emerged from various hiding places around them and began to approach cautiously. Among them was a second woman, also very pretty, with long, dark hair.

Luke turned back to Ursula and stared. Everything about her was utterly wonderful – from her sparkling sapphire eyes to her flawless skin and silky auburn hair. Long, black, perfectly manicured fingernails—

Luke rubbed his eyes. "You're under an enchantment charm!" he exclaimed. "You're a witch!"

"Morag and I are both witches," explained Ursula, gesturing towards her friend, who smiled at the new arrivals.

"This is incredible!" said Resus. "What are you all doing here?"

"Miss Ursula saved us!" cried a young banshee.

"Saved you?" said Luke. "Saved you from what?"

"Saved us from our dreams." A young ghost stepped forward and shook Luke's hand, sending shivers up and down his spine. "I'm Ryan," he said. "Miss

Ursula rescued us all – me, Addie, Jorden and the others. After *he* took us."

"I thought I'd never wake up again!" said the banshee.

"I was in bed in my cave – that's where he came for me!" shuddered a troll.

"That's what happened to our friend Cleo!" cried Resus. "Someone kidnapped her! We followed a trail of invisible goo to this jungle but didn't know where to go next."

"You can see the trails?" said Ursula, frowning. Then she gave Luke a smile. "Of course, you're a werewolf…"

Resus rubbed at the scratches on his hands. "Too bad he didn't think to transform when we were attacked by those ravens." The children gasped at the mention of the birds.

"Sounds like you've had a run-in with them too," said Luke.

"Are they coming, Miss Ursula?" cried Addie. "Is he back?"

"Of course not," the witch reassured her. "Spider will watch out for us, won't you?"

The ogre saluted. "Right away, Miss Ursula!" he declared. He took a step away from the group and shouted, "Power of a squirrel!" Then, with a cry of *"Chatter! Chatter!"* he scampered for the nearest tree and began to climb.

"That one suits him better," muttered Resus. "He's definitely nuts!"

"What's with the ravens?" Luke asked the two witches. "Why did they attack us?"

"It's not the ravens you need to worry about," Ursula replied. "They attack, yes, but they do it at his bidding; he won't have been far behind. That's why Spider got you away so quickly." They both ignored a spluttered cough from Resus.

"*His* bidding?" queried Luke. "I don't understand. *Who* won't be far behind?"

Ursula's voice trembled as she said the name. "The Nightwatchman."

Luke and Resus wanted to know more about the Nightwatchman, but Ursula insisted that they make camp first as the group had been walking all night.

Morag explained that the children had all been kidnapped from different G.H.O.U.L. communities. They were now searching the jungle for improvised Hex Hatches – like the one Luke and Resus had stumbled upon – in order to return to their homes. They travelled under cover of darkness, using what little moonlight filtered down through the trees to guide them.

Each of the children had a job to do, from collecting firewood to gathering food, all under the watchful gaze of Spider, who sat happily on an overhanging branch, gnawing on a twig.

Before long, the group was sitting around a small fire, talking contentedly as they feasted on nuts and berries.

"Tell us about the Nightwatchman," said Luke when they had finished eating. The other children fell silent.

"He's a dark, powerful creature," declared Ursula. "He steals children in the midst of their nightmares and brings them here to keep them asleep."

"Why would he keep them asleep?" asked Luke.

"The Nightwatchman feeds on terror," explained Ursula, "and there is no purer form than the fear a child experiences during a bad dream. The longer he keeps them in their nightmares, the more scared they become and the stronger he grows."

"But why only take kids from G.H.O.U.L. communities? There must be millions of normal children having nightmares every day."

"Normals might have frightening dreams about unusual life-forms such as vampires and werewolves," said Ursula. "Children like you, however, *start* their nightmares from that point, and they can only get worse."

Resus shuddered. "Do you think that's what happened to Cleo?" he asked. "She was having a nightmare and that attracted the Nightwatchman to her?"

"I'm certain of it," replied the witch. "Although you shouldn't have followed her here. You've both put yourselves in a lot of danger!"

"But Cleo's our friend," Luke said simply. "We came to rescue her, just like you've rescued all these kids."

"Each child's release was very dangerous," Ursula said. "It'll only be a matter of time before Morag and I are caught and punished by the Nightwatchman."

"Then why do you do it?" asked Luke.

Morag spoke up. "Because she cannot walk away," she explained. "She would not be Ursula Twist if she didn't try to rescue each and every child."

Luke's eyes widened. "Ursula *Twist*?" he gasped. "Are you any relation to a witch called Nelly Twist?"

Ursula looked surprised. "Nelly Twist is – was – my mother. She passed on from this world a long time ago."

"But we met her!" exclaimed Resus. "She came to life from the pages of a book and gave us

this!" He fumbled inside his cape and produced a vial of blood.

Ursula laughed. "Then I take it you have travelled here from Scream Street?"

Luke nodded. "We collected all six of the founding fathers' relics," he said. "But now I have to give them back to their original owners to try to reverse their magic – and I didn't know what to do with the witch's blood. Do you think it will work if I return it to you?"

"My mother's blood still flows through my veins," smiled Ursula. "I shall be delighted to accept her relic to aid your quest."

Resus handed Luke the bottle of blood. "Fancy meeting Nelly Twist's daughter," he beamed. "Every cloud has a silver lining, eh?"

"It certainly does!" growled a deep voice, and a sweaty hand yanked the vial away before Luke could take it. The boys spun round to see who had spoken.

It was Sir Otto Sneer.

Chapter Five
The Tower

Luke leapt over a fallen branch and began to chase Sir Otto Sneer through the lush under-growth, Resus just behind. "Something *did* follow us through the Hex Hatch," he wheezed. "It just wasn't a raven."

Despite his bulk, Sir Otto was pulling ahead. Smoke poured from the cigar in his mouth and trailed behind him like steam from a train.

Suddenly, Luke caught his foot on a tree root and crashed to the ground, taking Resus down

with him. By the time they had untangled them-selves, Scream Street's landlord was out of sight.

Luke cursed and kicked the tree that had tripped him up. "We've lost it!" he puffed, catching his breath. "The vial of witch's blood has gone!"

"Well, it's not exactly *gone*," said Resus. "We know who's got it."

"Yes, but how are we supposed to get it back?" snapped Luke.

"Sneer's bound to hide it somewhere in Scream Street," countered Resus. "We'll just have to search for it after we've rescued Cleo."

Reluctantly, Luke agreed and the boys returned to the witches' camp. By the time they arrived back, most of the children were curled up around the fire, asleep. Ursula looked up as they approached.

"We have to rescue Cleo," said Luke. "How long will it take us to get to wherever the Nightwatchman keeps his victims?"

"No time at all," Ursula assured him. "Look…" She led them to the edge of the clearing and parted the leaves to reveal a vast, black tower just a few metres away. The building rose

up, high above the tallest trees, jagged shards of metal jutting out from the top.

"That's impossible," protested Luke. "We climbed a tree and looked out over the jungle. We never saw a tower. There's no way we could have missed that!"

"It doesn't appear until after we've made camp," explained Ursula, "and then it's always right behind us, no matter how far we've travelled. Each night we walk for miles, and the next morning – there's the tower."

"But that means… That means the tower is *following* you!" spluttered Resus.

"Yes," said Ursula. "Which is another reason the children sleep during the day. My powers can protect them while the sun's up, but when darkness falls, the Nightwatchman's magic is much stronger than mine."

"You *are* rescuing the children, aren't you?" asked Resus. "From inside the tower…"

"Not quickly enough," replied Ursula fervently. "For every child I save, he takes two from their beds. It's a losing battle – but I can't give up."

Luke stared up at the imposing structure. "So you think Cleo's inside there, right now?"

Ursula nodded. "Yes, if the Nightwatchman took her."

"Then we're going in."

Ursula and Spider led the boys around the base of the tower. Luke put his hands out and

touched the rough stonework, but then quickly pulled them away again. "It has the same effect as the blood," he said with a shiver. "You feel like life isn't worth living."

"Don't let the feeling overwhelm you, or he'll win," urged Ursula, staring intently at him. "You have to remember that life *is* worth living."

"Yeah," agreed Resus, "but it's worth living a long way away from here!"

"There it is, Miss Ursula," announced Spider, pointing to a small metal grid set in the wall near the top of the tower.

Luke squinted up to try to get a better view. "What *is* that?" he asked.

"A ventilation grille," replied Ursula. "And our only way inside."

Resus laughed. "Now I *know* everyone's mad," he said. "Even if we manage to get up there, we'll have to be chopped into little pieces and posted through – it's tiny!"

"That's how we get in every time we rescue another child, and so far the Nightwatchman hasn't realized how we're doing it," Ursula assured him.

Resus peered up at the metal hatch. "You get in up *there*?"

"Spider can climb the tower," the witch explained. Then she raised her hand to show black sparks fizzing around her fingers. "And I do have one or two tricks up my sleeve!"

"Why do I not like the sound of where this is going?" groaned Resus.

"I can cast a spell to miniaturize you both," said Ursula. "Once Spider is level with the venti-lation shaft, he'll simply slip you inside."

"Miniaturize us?" exclaimed Resus. "What are we supposed to do when we get inside? Bite the Nightwatchman on the toe?"

"The spell is temporary," Ursula assured him, "designed to wear off after a short while. When you're ready to come back out, use this…" She handed Luke a magic wand with a black star on the end. "It's pre-loaded with a single spell – and it will shrink you and your friend just long enough to allow you all to escape. I'll make sure Spider is waiting for you on the other side."

"OK," said Luke, tucking the wand under his arm. "Let's do it!" He stood beside Resus as

Ursula began to mutter a spell over them.

Luke's mind swam and a bizarre feeling began to wash over him. It felt a bit like the start of one of his transformations, only without the sensation of rage. Ursula and Spider were suddenly growing – no, it was he and Resus who were shrinking! The boys became smaller and smaller until they had to stand on tiptoe to see over the blades of grass. The wand Luke was clutching had shrunk with them.

"Everything had better grow back to its proper size or Cleo's gonna be in even *more* trouble when I get hold of her," squeaked Resus. "I sound like a chipmunk!"

Luke laughed, and discovered that his own voice was no better. "It's only for a short time," he said.

"Don't say *short*!" peeped Resus.

Spider bent down to collect the tiny boys in his hands. "Aww…" he grinned. "They looks so cute!"

Resus glared up at the massive ogre face that filled his vision. "Well, *you* don't!" he responded. "When was the last time you blew your nose?"

Ursula smiled at Luke and Resus. "Now listen," she said, "neither of you will be able to break the Nightwatchman's sleeping spell — only your friend has the power to do that. She'll have to try to find the strength inside herself."

"She's strong," Luke assured the witch.

"You'd better hurry, Spider," Ursula instructed. "They don't have long before the spell wears off."

"Yes, Miss Ursula," said the ogre, tucking the boys into his pocket. He stepped back from the tower, shouted "Power of a monkey!" and began to wave his arms around once more.

"Here he goes," muttered Resus, watching the fake transformation from the viewpoint of Spider's chest. "The Amazing Spider-Fraud!"

Luke nudged his friend. "So he's a little unusual…"

"Don't say *little*, either!"

When Spider's gyrations were over, the ogre spat on his hands and clamped them to the stonework of the tower. *"Ooh! Ooh! Aah! Aah!"* he yelled, chimp-like, then began to climb.

"How's he doing that?" asked Luke.

"Ogre spit," replied Resus. "Strongest natural glue in the world. Just about the only thing it doesn't stick to permanently is the ogre itself."

Luke watched as Spider dragged his first hand away from the wall, the thick saliva stretching out until finally it snapped. "This could take a while," he said.

"It would be a lot quicker if he didn't keep pausing to scratch his armpits and pretend to eat bananas," added Resus.

Steadily, Spider climbed hand over hand until the boys were level with the ventilation shaft. "OK, little fellas," the ogre huffed, clinging on tightly.

Resus cupped his hands and gave the tiny figure of Luke a lift up to the edge of the grille. Luke reached down to pull his friend up after him.

"May the powers of the animals go with you, my darlings," smiled Spider as he began to slide back down to the ground.

Resus leant through the grille to watch him go. "I think we've got more chance than you on that one," he peeped. Ducking back into the shaft, he followed Luke into the gloom.

The ventilation tunnel was old and dirty.

Stale air wafted around them as the boys climbed over piles of dust the size of sand dunes, heading deeper into the tower. The tunnel sloped steadily downwards, and a dim light could be seen glowing at the far end. The boys hurried towards it.

Eventually they reached a second grille. Peering through, they found themselves overlooking a large dormitory. Dozens of rusted metal bedsteads stood in rows on the bare floorboards, and strapped to each was a sleeping child.

"It looks like it's going to take us a while to find Cleo," Resus gulped.

Click!

Luke frowned at Resus. "What did you do that for?"

"Do what?"

"Make that funny clicking noise."

"I didn't," said Resus.

Click!

"There! You did it again!" insisted Luke.

"That wasn't me!"

"Then who was it?"

Click!

The boys slowly turned and looked back

where they had come from. Crawling towards
them was a very large beetle.

Chapter Six
The Dormitory

The beetle was racing towards Luke and Resus, razor-sharp pincers snapping angrily like the jaws of a shark. To the boys in their current size, it was as big as a dog.

"We've got to get out of here!" yelled Resus.

Luke peered through the grille at the dormitory far below. "How?" he demanded. "If we jump, we'll be flattened!"

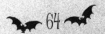

"And if we stay, we'll be dinner!"

Suddenly, Luke spotted something fine and silky dangling from the ceiling, just the other side of the grille. An old cobweb. "There!" he shouted. "Now!"

Luke and Resus squeezed through the bars, took a flying leap into the room and managed to grab onto the strand of web just as the beetle crashed into the metal grille behind them. They swung out across the room, Luke still clutching the wand.

Resus glanced back at the furious beetle as it hissed and snapped at them. "We did it!" he cried. "We escaped!"

Then the cobweb snapped.

The boys fell, tumbling through the air for what seemed an age before landing on something rough, white and scratchy. They lay still, trying to catch their breath.

"I'm never listening to your crazy ideas ever again," grunted Resus.

"It was only *my crazy idea* that stopped us from being sliced and diced by beetle-saurus back there!" hissed Luke. "Now quit your whining and start thinking of a way to get down from here.

We need to hide until the spell wears off."

Resus stuck his tongue out behind Luke's back. "When I'm normal size again," he said, looking around him to try to get his bearings, "I'm going to stamp on every beetle I—"

He froze, a look of astonishment on his face.

"What?" asked Luke.

Resus gestured from the long stretch of stomach bandage they were standing on to the gigantic sleeping mummy's face at the other end of the bed.

"I think we've found Cleo."

Ten minutes later, Luke and Resus were returning to their natural size. They had unwound a portion of bandage from Cleo's arm and used it to climb to the floor, where they hid under the bed until the miniaturization spell began to wear off.

When the bizarre growing feeling finally abated, they slid out from beneath the rusting metal frame. Luke had just slipped the wand into the back pocket of his jeans when a series of screams echoed around the dormitory.

First a young zombie in the bed nearest the door began to thrash about and screech in terror, then a skeleton took up the cry, followed by the troll next to him. The scream appeared to be travelling around the room.

"They're having the same nightmare!" exclaimed Luke. "The dream is passing from one kid to the next!"

"Then let's get Cleo out of here before it reaches her!" cried Resus, shaking the mummy's shoulder. "Come on, Cleo. Wakey, wakey, rise and shine!"

But the mummy remained sound asleep – and the moving nightmare was now just a few beds

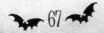

away. "It's not working," said Resus. "I can't wake her up!"

Luke looked on as the dream reached Cleo and she too began to scream, straining against the straps that bound her to the bed frame. Her eyes snapped open for a moment and stared directly at her friends, but she didn't seem to see them.

Luke picked up her hand and squeezed it tightly. "It's OK," he whispered. "Resus and I are here!" Suddenly, the bog monster in the next bed began to writhe around in fear, and the nightmare left Cleo just as quickly as it had arrived. The mummy slumped back against the rusty springs, her bandages soaked with sweat.

"Well, if that didn't wake her, nothing will," sighed Resus.

"Ursula said we won't be able to break the sleeping spell ourselves," Luke reminded him, lowering the mummy's hand gently back onto the bed. "Only Cleo has the power to do that."

"The problem is – how do we tell *her* that?"

"I think I might know," said Luke, spotting two empty beds at the far end of the dormitory. He grabbed Resus's arm and led him towards them. "Do you ever have those dreams where you literally scare yourself awake?"

"All the time," the vampire replied. "Last week I dreamt that I had bunk beds and Sir Otto had moved in with me. I woke up wrestling my pillow."

Luke nodded. "It was something inside the dream that woke you," he said, lying down on one of the free beds. "I reckon the only chance we have of getting Cleo out of here is to wake her from the inside."

Resus stared as Luke stuffed a grotty, ragged pillow under his head. "Wait – you want us to go inside a nightmare and rescue Cleo that way?"

Luke began to fasten the straps across his chest. "Think about it," he said. "That *must* be how Ursula's doing it. Besides, this is Cleo. We've been through some terrifying stuff together – I'm sure we can cope with her bad dreams."

"What about that moving nightmare?" demanded Resus. "The one that's just had every-one screaming like a banshee with its finger trapped in a coffin?"

Luke tightened the buckle of his strap. "We'll just have to hope we get out before it comes back again."

"Except that when it does, we'll be trapped!" countered Resus. "Why have you strapped yourself to the bed anyway?"

"If the Nightwatchman comes around, he might become suspicious if two of his captives are untied," explained Luke.

"The *Nightwatchman*?" Resus spluttered. "This gets worse by the second!"

"Don't worry, we probably won't see him," said Luke. "Now, get into bed."

Grumbling, Resus lay down on the bed next to Luke and pulled his own straps across his chest. "I remember when the most exciting thing that ever happened to me was when I accidentally bit through a toothbrush with my fangs."

"You'll never get to sleep if you keep talking…"

Resus gazed up at the peeling paint above him and shifted his back to avoid the sharp springs of the bed frame. "Yeah, 'cos that's the only thing stopping me from dropping off," he muttered. But he obediently closed his eyes and tried to relax.

Luke was surprised at how quickly he began to feel drowsy. Whether it was the effect of the

sleeping spell he guessed lay over the room or the fact that he'd been woken up so early by Kian, his eyelids soon began to feel heavy.

"How are you doing?" he called quietly to Resus – but the vampire was already asleep, snoring softly.

Luke smiled and allowed the tiredness to wash over him …

… then jumped at the sound of music. It was a tinkling tune, the kind played by his mum's jewellery box at home. Luke sat up to discover that he was no longer strapped to his bed.

Swinging his feet to the floor, he reached over and shook Resus awake. The vampire opened his eyes and blinked. "What's happening?" he asked.

"I don't know," replied Luke, "but we seem to be alone. Everyone else has gone!"

Resus sat up and looked around the now deserted dormitory. "How long have we been asleep?" he said. "I didn't manage to get inside Cleo's dream. Did you?"

Luke shook his head. "Well, it was worth a try."

"So, what do we do now?" Resus demanded in frustration. "It's not like we can just…" He

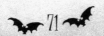

71

paused and ran his tongue over his gums. "Hang on…"

"What?" asked Luke.

Resus gripped hold of a sharp tooth and pulled. "My fangs," he breathed. "They're not fake any more. They're real!"

A crooning voice could be heard over the music. Following the sound, Luke looked up at the ventilation shaft to see the beetle, now dressed in a top hat and tails, singing along. The insect winked at him.

"We've done it!" exclaimed Luke. "We've fallen asleep, and we're dreaming!"

In a flash of black smoke, Resus transformed into a bat and flapped up into the air.

"What makes you say that?" he joked excitedly.

Grinning, Luke grabbed his friend and pulled him down from the ceiling, where he changed back to vampire form. "Now we just have to find Cleo."

"Where do we start?"

Luke gestured towards a nearby door. "Follow the music!"

The staircase was old and rotten, but Luke discovered that he could repair it just by staring at each step in turn. This dreaming lark wasn't so bad after all!

Before long, the boys arrived at an identical dormitory on the floor below. However, here the beds had been pushed back against the walls and a table in the middle of the room had been set out with teacups and cakes. Seated around the table were a handful of ragdolls ... and Cleo.

"There she is!" cried Resus, and he dashed across the room to his friend – stopping in his tracks when Cleo snapped her head up and gave him a glare.

"Stay back!" the mummy commanded. "Don't come near me!"

Chapter Seven
The Mummy's Dream

Luke stared at Cleo. "I don't understand," he said. "Why don't you want us here? We've entered this dream to help you!"

"It's not just any dream," said Cleo. "It's *my* dream. My worst nightmare, to be exact. You're not safe here!"

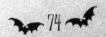

Resus studied the tea party and frowned. "*This* is your worst nightmare? Playing with dolls?"

"And wearing this!" added Cleo. She stood to reveal a frilly pink dress and a white lace pinafore. On her feet were a pair of sparkly silver shoes.

Resus bit his tongue with one of his new-found fangs in an effort not to laugh. "It suits you," he said.

"No more than it suits you," retorted Cleo crossly.

Resus looked down at his clothes to discover that his black vampire cape had gone, and in its place was a pale blue party frock. "Whoa!" he yelled.

Luke, now dressed in a blouse and skirt, raced over to the table, blue ribbons bobbing in his hair. "It doesn't matter what we're wearing,"

he declared. "It's just a dream – and we have to find a way out of here, now!" But before he could pull Cleo away, the table jolted towards him and knocked him off his feet. He sat down heavily in one of the chairs.

"Don't you think I've *tried* to get out of here?" Cleo said sadly. "Every time I make a move, the tea party drags me back in."

"That's ridiculous!" barked Resus as lipstick and blusher suddenly appeared over his pale features. Then another of the chairs suddenly flew up in the air, circled the room and dragged the vampire to the table.

"Then again, I can see your problem," he added.

Cleo picked up the teapot and got ready to pour. "We have to go through with this – or *he* comes and makes things worse."

"He?" hissed Luke. "You mean … the Nightwatchman?"

Cleo nodded, her eyes flicking towards the door. "Try not to mention his name," she shuddered. "It's bad enough when he turns up unannounced."

"But didn't you hurt him?" said Resus,

remembering. "We saw the trail of blood leading from your bedroom – well, Luke did, anyway."

"Blood?" asked Cleo.

"Blood," Resus confirmed. "You know, the stuff my dad uses in cocktails."

"Do you mean this?" Reaching up, Cleo grabbed the light fitting above her head and directed it towards the wall, revealing splashes of the same green goo the boys had followed from Scream Street.

Luke nodded, realizing he could see the stuff without his werewolf vision now he was inside the dream. "That's it," he gulped.

"That's not blood," whispered Cleo. "That's terror – *my* terror! The stuff the Nightwatchman feeds on."

Resus's eyes widened. "So that's why we felt so sad when we touched it," he gasped. "We were feeling *your* fear!"

"Exactly," said Cleo. "I was having a nightmare back at home when I felt something dark and shadowy coming towards me. I jumped out of bed in my sleep and locked my bedroom door."

"Which explains why the Nightwatchman had to break in," said Luke.

"And why he keeps the kids strapped to those old beds in the dormitories," added Resus. "He doesn't want them trying to fight back – even in their sleep."

"But there must be a way out of this dream," insisted Luke, "even if you're being kept asleep by magic. People don't suffer through their worst nightmare every night. They dream about other things too. Before Kian woke me this morning, I was watching meerkats performing on a trapeze!"

"Maybe you just have to reject this dream and move on to the next one," suggested Resus. "You know – choose something else to dream about."

Cleo looked thoughtful. "I suppose I could give it a go," she said. Gritting her teeth, she snatched up one of the ragdolls and hurled it across the room. "Get away from us!" she bellowed. The doll bounced off the wall and fell to the floor.

"Brilliant!" beamed Resus. "That was easy enough. Now, let's get out of these stupid dresses and we can—"

The ragdoll slowly turned its head and looked at the trio.

"Uh-oh…"

Climbing to its knitted feet, the doll steadily plodded back towards Cleo, singing in a high, off-key voice,

"Ring-a-ring o' roses,
You're wearing girly clothes-es…"

The other dolls joined in the chant and began to close in around the mummy.

"For ever! For ever!
You'll always play with ussssssss!"

 79

"Get them away from me!" Cleo shrieked as the dolls began to clamber over her.

Luke pulled the first one away from his friend, and in desperation he ripped it in half before tossing it aside. But the legs simply jumped up and ran back to the battle while the upper half followed, pulling itself across the floorboards.

Resus swung his leg round and kicked another of the tiny monsters across the room, sending it crashing into a box of play jewellery. The doll re-emerged, hurling brooches and hairclips at him as though they were ninja throwing stars.

Dozens more ragdolls dragged themselves out from under beds and lurched towards Cleo. The mummy was slowly disappearing beneath them.

"Little Miss Mummy lay on her tummy,
Dreaming of beads and pearls…"

A larger, walking-talking doll appeared in the doorway and tottered forward unsteadily, its eyes shining as it sang,

"Along came a dolly that made her feel jolly
And now she's just one of the girls!"

"You have to stop this yourself!" Luke shouted to Cleo. "There's nothing Resus or I can do!"

"But how?" came Cleo's muffled voice. "I

never played with dolls – I always thought they were childish."

"Then *be* that person!" roared Luke. "Forget about them and grow up!"

With a supreme effort, Cleo pushed enough of the dolls to one side to allow her to sit up. She tore at her party dress. "I don't play with dolls!" she yelled angrily. "I fight Hellhounds, tunnel with zombies and rescue bog monsters from slime-filled swimming pools."

"Mama! Mama!" The walking doll was almost upon her.

"I don't like girls' toys," Cleo bawled. "I'm a TOMBOY!"

The woollen figures paused in their assault, their faces twisted in fear. Even the larger doll seemed to falter for a second.

"Mama?"

"You lot are nothing but a waste of wool," Cleo continued. The dolls began to edge away from her.

"Keep going!" encouraged Resus.

Cleo finally stood and ripped off what remained of her dress. "And I'll tell you another thing," she yelled. "I NEVER liked tea!" She

grabbed the teapot from the table, spun round and used it like a watering can to spray the liquid across everything and everyone in the room. As soon as it hit the dolls, they began to melt away, their cries echoing around the dormitory. Soon they were all gone.

Resus wiped tea from his face and hugged Cleo excitedly. "You were brilliant!" he beamed.

Cleo held the vampire at arm's length and pretended to be cross. "You two certainly took your time," she complained. "What happened? Was there a new issue of the *Illustrated Idiot* you had to read before you could set off on your rescue mission?"

Resus grinned. "Well, at least there don't seem to be any lasting effects…"

"My dress has disappeared!" Luke exclaimed, looking down to discover he was back in jeans and a T-shirt.

Resus twirled his cape. "And I look like a vampire again," he grinned.

"*Looking* like a vampire means nothing!" announced a deep voice from somewhere behind them.

Cleo jumped as the room began to change

around them, the walls falling away to reveal a vast stone chamber. "What's going on?" she exclaimed.

Two adult vampires appeared behind Resus. One of them pulled his hands behind his back and secured them with handcuffs.

"Resus Negative," pronounced the second. "You are under arrest for impersonating a vampire!"

Chapter Eight

The Vampire's Dream

"No!" Luke ran forward to help Resus, but one of the vampires stepped in his way.

"If you wish to remain in court, you will have to take a seat, sir!" he growled.

Luke stared around him. They were now in a large but dimly lit cavern filled with battered

wooden benches, ageing varnish peeling from the dark surfaces. He and Cleo were ushered into seats behind a large desk marked Witnesses.

Resus, meanwhile, struggled as the first vampire pushed him inside a small, metal cage and swung the door shut with a *clang*. "What are you doing? Let me go!" he cried.

A chorus of cheers and applause rang out above them as the cage was locked. Luke looked up to see a balcony running all the way around the room, crammed with excited vampires of all shapes and sizes.

Cleo clutched Luke's arm, trembling. "What's happening?" she whispered. "What *is* this place?"

Luke tried to keep his own voice from shaking. "I think we're inside *Resus's* worst nightmare now," he gulped.

"All rise for His Honour, Judge Mortis!" a voice boomed.

Cleo and Luke were pushed to their feet as an elderly vampire entered the room. He was dressed in black robes and a white wig, and his fangs were twisted and gnarled, blood dripping from them as though he had just fed. The audience in the balcony cooed with delight.

 85

Judge Mortis glared at Resus. "Is this the accused?" he grunted, licking the tips of his twisted fangs.

"This is he," one of the guards replied, saluting smartly.

"Then we begin." He picked up a wooden gavel and rapped it on his desk. "Court is now in session!"

Luke and Cleo sat back down. Resus gripped the bars of his cage and peered miserably through.

"Resus Stoker Negative..." rumbled the judge.

"*Stoker?*" whispered Cleo.

Judge Mortis banged his gavel again. "There will be silence in court!" he roared.

Cleo shrank down in her seat and the judge turned back to glare at the accused. "Resus Stoker Negative, you are charged with impersonating a vampire and living with a true vampire family, even though you are nothing but a *normal*!" He spat out the final word and the vampires in the balcony gave out a theatrical *"Ooh!"*.

"But I *am* a vampire!" yelled Resus. "I'm not impersonating anything!"

"Then prove it," growled the judge. "Show the court your fangs."

A look of hope crossed Resus's face. Since he had been dreaming, his fangs had been real. "Here!" he cried, opening his mouth wide.

Judge Mortis thrust his hand through the bars of the cage and grabbed hold of Resus's teeth. He pulled hard and yanked the fangs out of the young vampire's mouth, revealing a row of ordinary teeth behind.

Luke gasped. "His fangs! They're fake again!"

The crowd leaning over the edge of the balcony booed and hissed.

 87

Resus put his hand to his mouth. "They *were* real!" he exclaimed.

Judge Mortis held Resus's fake fangs up to the light. "Then explain to the court why you wear these cheap imitations!" he bellowed.

Tears began to well up in Resus's eyes. "I… I can't…"

"Strike one," declared the judge, and the audience burst into applause.

The judge tossed the fangs back into the cage. "Guard!" he yelled as Resus scrabbled about on the floor to retrieve them. "Fetch me a mirror!"

"Oh no," said Luke.

"What's wrong?" Cleo asked.

"They're going to check if Resus has a reflection!"

"Why? Doesn't everybody?"

"Not vampires," replied Luke. "Well, real vampires, anyway."

The guard reappeared with a hand mirror, which he held in front of the cage. Judge Mortis leant over to peer at where Resus's reflection shouldn't be…

"I can see him!" the judge shrieked. "This so-called vampire has a *reflection*! Strike two!"

The crowd in the balcony went crazy, hurling insults and, in one case, even rotten fruit at the cage. Resus shrank back as far as he could, tears now running freely down his face.

Judge Mortis rapped his gavel again. "Silence!" he demanded. "We have one final test to undertake." He glared at Resus. "If you are, as you claim, a true vampire … then you will not object to drinking blood."

One of the guards produced a goblet full of crimson liquid. The audience of vampires hissed and licked their lips.

"No!" Resus sobbed. "Please…"

"Drink!" the judge ordered.

Resus took the goblet in trembling fingers and slowly raised it to his lips. His fangs tinkled against the edge of the glass.

The gallery held its collective breath.

"I won't do it!" screamed Resus suddenly, hurling the goblet to the floor of the cage, where it smashed, spraying blood everywhere.

"He will not drink!" bellowed the judge. "Strike three!"

The watching vampires leapt to their feet and began to cheer wildly.

Judge Mortis hammered his gavel repeatedly until silence filled the courtroom once more. "Resus Stoker Negative," he announced, "you have been found guilty of impersonating a vampire. You shall spend the remainder of your days in the Underlands."

"This isn't fair!" shouted Luke, jumping to his feet. "I demand to speak on Resus's behalf!"

The judge turned to glare at Luke. "And who," he gurgled, "are you?"

"My name is Luke Watson, and I'm Resus's friend."

Judge Mortis sneered. "As delighted as we all are to discover that the faker has an acquaintance, my judgment has been passed!"

"But this box says Witnesses," insisted Luke. "And you haven't called for any! I don't know much about vampire law, but I'm pretty certain you're allowed to defend yourselves openly and fairly."

Hushed whispers could be heard in the gallery as Judge Mortis considered Luke's words. "Very well," he said finally, "you may attempt to defend the accused – but if you fail you shall *both* be banished to the Underlands!"

"Make that three of us!" cried Cleo, standing beside Luke.

Judge Mortis began to laugh mockingly. "It seems you are quite the heroes," he sneered. "So be it. The mummy shall go first."

A guard dragged Cleo to stand beside the cage. She reached through the bars and took Resus's hand, giving it a squeeze.

A vampire in a suit approached them. "State your name."

"Cleopatra Farr, former handmaiden to Queen Nefertari of Egypt."

"Miss Farr, how long have you known this 'vampire'?"

"Ever since I moved to Scream Street," Cleo declared. "And it doesn't matter what you say about his reflection, or the fact that he doesn't like the taste of blood – he *is* a real vampire. Look!"

She pulled Resus's hand through the bars of the cage and held it, palm up, towards the judge. "Study the lines," Cleo directed. "Resus is descended from the glorious line of Count Negatov himself!"

The gallery vampires cried out in disgust at the claim.

Judge Mortis silenced them, then removed his spectacles to study Resus's palm. "Is this some sort of joke, young lady?" he asked.

"Of course not!" retorted Cleo. "The lines clearly show—"

She looked down and froze. Resus's palm was completely smooth and bare. "I-I don't understand…"

"Remove her," ordered the judge as Resus lowered his head in dismay.

"No!" yelled Cleo as one of the guards approached. "His palm usually shows he's a Negative, I've seen it!" The guard picked her up and carried her across the courtroom, dumping her back down beside Luke.

"It's OK," he whispered to her. "I know what to do."

Luke made his way over to the witness stand and stood facing the suited vampire. "My name is Luke Thomas Watson, and I'm a werewolf," he proclaimed.

The lawyer indicated Resus's cage. "Do you deny that this boy is a normal?"

"Not at all," Luke replied. The audience gasped. "Resus Negative *is* a normal," Luke

continued, "but a normal born to true vampire parents. He might have to wear fake fangs and dye his hair, but he will prove his heritage by acting like each and every one of you."

He pulled down the collar of his T-shirt, pressed his neck against the bars of the cage and hissed, "Bite me!"

Resus stared at his friend, white-faced. "B-but, Luke…"

"It's just a dream," Luke insisted through gritted teeth. "Now, bite me!"

Resus slowly leant forward…

Luke closed his eyes and felt the sharp points begin to press against his skin…

Then Cleo screamed.

Luke's eyes snapped open. The courtroom had vanished – he was back in his house in Scream Street. And it wasn't Resus who was biting his neck.

It was his mum.

The Werewolf's Dream

Luke stared at his mum in horror and pulled away. She was halfway through her werewolf transformation, long talons sliding through her fingertips. The two of them were in a room that looked exactly like their living room at home.

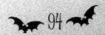

"It's just a dream!" Luke told himself urgently. A noise made him jump, and he looked up to see Cleo and Resus outside, hammering on the living-room window.

"It's *not* just a dream!" Cleo yelled. "It's your worst nightmare, created for you by the Nightwatchman – if you die here, you die in real life!"

Resus stared at her. "And when were you going to tell us this?" he demanded.

The mummy shrieked in frustration. "Didn't you two do *any* research about this place before you came bumbling in?"

Inside the room, Mrs Watson threw her head back and howled as her face stretched to form a snout, and blonde fur began to cover her body. Luke ran for the door – but it was locked.

"No!" he pleaded, his fists pounding against the wood. "Please don't make me go through this!"

The sound of cracking bones made him turn to see his mum's spine reshape, and the fully formed werewolf begin to stalk across the room towards him.

"Luke!" Cleo yelled, her face pressed against

the window. "You have to transform. You have to fight!"

"I-I can't," stammered Luke from his position by the door. "I can't fight my own mum."

"She's *not* your mum," countered Resus. "She's just part of this nightmare and *looks* like your mum."

"Unless, of course, Mrs Watson is asleep at the moment and having the exact same nightmare," said Cleo thoughtfully. "Then I suppose it could be his mum…"

"You really know how to put a damper on things, don't you," barked Resus. The vampire pressed his own face against the glass. "OK, the chances are good that she's *not* your mum!" he shouted.

With a roar, the blonde werewolf pounced. Luke threw himself to the ground, the creature's jaws snapping shut just centimetres from his face. The beast lashed out with a paw and caught his arm, delivering a deep, painful cut.

Luke half crawled, half scrabbled his way across the carpet, trying to put as many items of furniture as he could between himself and the wolf. "Please, mum," he begged. "Please stop this!"

"Luke! You have to fight back!" bellowed Resus.

Catching sight of him and Cleo outside, the werewolf leapt at the window with a snarl, its claws dragging down the glass and squealing like chalk on a blackboard.

Luke clutched at his injured arm. Blood seeped through his fingertips and ran over the back of his hand. The werewolf darted forward again and bit down hard on his ankle as he tried to dodge the attack. Pain shot up his leg and he crashed to the ground, his hands held out to protect him from the gnashing teeth.

Somehow, over the furious growling of the wolf, Luke could hear Cleo's voice shouting at him. "You have to put an end to this *now*! He's coming!"

Luke turned his head to look up at the window. A storm was building outside. Resus's cape flapped in a raging gale as dark clouds rolled in at an absurd pace. Rain began to pelt down, soaking his friends, and there were crashes of thunder... No, not thunder – voices.

Children's voices, screaming for help.

The Nightwatchman's dream was rolling

towards them again.

Luke suddenly became aware that streaks of pulsing green goo covered every surface, and he stared at his own fear. He had to keep that fear and anger from taking over his mind. If he transformed, he would almost certainly fight back – and there was no knowing what he would do then. He couldn't let that happen.

He found the strength to pull away from the creature and drag himself across the carpet to take refuge beneath the coffee table. The werewolf followed, snarling as it crashed on top of the table and clawed at the polished surface.

Outside the window, barely able to stay on their feet in the raging thunderstorm, Resus and Cleo couldn't believe what they were seeing.

"He's not transforming!" Cleo bellowed over the sound of the pelting rain. "She's going to hurt him!"

"Luke – do something!" urged Resus.

Luke took a deep breath. His friends were right – it was time for action. Pulling himself to his feet, he turned to face the werewolf once again. "I know you're not my mum!" he shouted. "I'm not scared of you!"

The werewolf leapt towards him. Luke screwed up his eyes and waited for the impact – but it didn't come. Instead, the howling of the wind and the echoing mournful cries were joined by the sound of rhythmic tapping.

Cautiously, Luke opened his eyes and was astonished to find the room suddenly filled with performing ravens. There were some on the sofa riding tiny unicycles, a pair of them in leotards were swinging from the light fitting and a group near the fireplace were performing the dance routine from his dream the night before. There was no sign of his mum, and the trails of sticky, green fear had begun to fade.

Outside, Cleo and Resus were screaming again – but this time with joy. They hugged each other tightly, daring to believe that the nightmare might finally be over. Luke turned to face them through the rain-spattered glass and took a deep bow.

Then there came an almighty shriek. As one, the ravens had launched themselves into the air and were now flying up to the ceiling, cawing madly.

Luke ducked, but the birds weren't interested in him. They flew in a tighter and tighter circle until they seemed to melt together, forming a single shape. It could have been human – but only the kind of human found in a nightmare world such as this. The figure grew, blocking out the light from the window. Matted hair clung to its flaking scalp and piercing white eyes flashed as they scanned the room.

Luke gasped. He was sure he had seen this monster before. Was it the shape that had followed him when he fell from the tree in the jungle? Terror overtook him as he suddenly realized it was the Nightwatchman himself.

"So, you choose not to play my little game?"

the Nightwatchman growled. His voice was so deep, Luke could feel it rumbling in the very core of his bones. "Your own worst nightmare, and you refuse to be scared by it…"

"I refuse to be scared by *you*," retorted Luke, hoping his trembling hands wouldn't give him away. "I won't let you do this any more!"

The Nightwatchman threw back his head and laughed. The sound was more hideous and more terrifying than anything Luke had witnessed so far. On the other side of the window, Resus and Cleo shuddered and clung to one another.

"You seek to challenge me, boy?" hissed the creature.

"I'll do more than challenge you," Luke declared bravely. "I'll stop you!"

The Nightwatchman exploded back into a hundred ravens. The birds flew across the room and reformed behind Luke.

"You do not alarm me, child," said the Nightwatchman. "I feed on your kind; feed on the fear that I know exists within you."

Luke spun to face his tormentor. "This is nothing but a bad dream," he insisted. "There's no fear inside me."

 102

"We shall see…" rumbled the Nightwatchman. He clicked his fingers, and in another flash of lightning, the walls of 13 Scream Street fell away. Wind and rain lashed at Luke's face and he fought to retain his balance.

He and the Nightwatchman were suddenly back in the jungle, standing on the roof of the black tower, twisted shards of metal scraping the sky above. Resus and Cleo stood huddled together just a few metres away.

"*I* shall show you fear," growled the Nightwatchman, peering down at Luke with his pulsing white eyes. "I shall show you TERROR!"

And in one swift movement, he shot out a long, black arm, snatched up Resus and Cleo, and threw them over the edge of the tower.

Chapter Ten
The Escape

Luke raced towards where his friends had disappeared, but the Nightwatchman blocked his way.

Luke glared up at the shadowy figure. "You monster," he spat.

The Nightwatchman bowed slightly, pleased with the compliment. "Tell me you have no fear now, boy!"

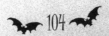

Luke tried to fight the terror building up inside him, but it was no use. What if Cleo and Resus had died inside this nightmare? If Cleo's theory was correct, his friends would never wake again.

And it would all be his fault.

Sadness flooded every cell in Luke's body. He wanted to drop to his knees and cry, but he didn't want to give the Nightwatchman the satisfaction.

Then he heard something – a distant voice, carried up by the wind. He began to laugh.

The Nightwatchman's eyes flashed with anger. "Are you mad, boy?"

Luke's laughter grew and grew.

"Stop it!" roared the Nightwatchman, clutching at his stomach.

So strong was his laughter, Luke was wiping tears from the corners of his eyes. He'd got the giggles and simply couldn't stop.

The Nightwatchman was now bent double in pain. "Stop this, now!" he screamed. "I brought you here to feed on your fear!"

Luke grinned up at him. "If it's my fear you're after," he chuckled, "then I guess you're about to go on a diet!" And, with a wink, he ran past the Nightwatchman and leapt off the roof of the tower.

 105

Luke landed in the spiderweb next to Cleo. The mummy was trying to untangle herself from the sticky gossamer that was stretched between two trees a couple of metres above the ground.

"You're alive!" she squealed, giving him a hug.

"So are you!" beamed Luke, catching sight of Resus standing beside the makeshift net. They both jumped to the ground.

Spider came lumbering over. "I used the power of a spider that time, Master Luke," he said proudly.

"I know," said Luke. "I heard you telling Resus just after the Nightwatchman threw them off the roof – and I suddenly realized what Ursula had meant when she said you'd be waiting for us on the other side. You're asleep too, aren't you?"

"Snoring like a good 'un!" grinned Spider. "Being a spider is my favourite – and I made the web myself."

Cleo peered up at the thick, black hair covering Spider's chest. "You made it your— *Eurgh!*"

"Never mind that," said Luke, taking his friends by the hands. "What matters now is that we all have to WAKE UP!"

Luke and Resus snapped awake at exactly the same moment. They were still in the dormitory, along with all the other children. Further down the row of beds, Cleo was groggily trying to sit up.

Luke whipped off his straps and hurried over to help the mummy. She swung her legs off the bed and clutched at her head. "So, it's true," she said. "You two really were in my dream?"

"Yep," said Resus, joining them. "Got thrown off the tower with you and everything!"

"Then how did we wake up?" Cleo asked. "Why are we awake and all the other kids still asleep?"

"Maybe it's because we faced up to our worst nightmares and survived," suggested Luke. "Everyone else is still suffering through theirs again and again."

Resus shuddered.

"And if we don't want to go back there, we'd better get going," Luke added. "The Nightwatchman won't stand for being tricked like that." He pulled the magic wand from his pocket and frowned. It had snapped in two.

"Oh no," breathed Resus.

"What's wrong?" asked Cleo. "What's that?"

"Our way out of here," sighed the vampire. He tried holding the two halves of the wand together and waved it over Cleo's head – but nothing happened.

"Hang on a minute…" Luke dashed over to the bed where the young zombie lay sleeping and unfastened his straps.

"What are you doing?" demanded Cleo.

108

"There are hundreds of kids in here – we don't have time to untie them all!"

"We don't need to," Luke assured her. "Just one."

Suddenly the door at the other end of the room swung shut. "Well, what do you know?" smirked Resus. "I think the tower wants to play with us." He produced the chainsaw from beneath his cloak. "Just as well I'm good at this game…"

Firing it up, the vampire plunged the power tool deep into the door, reducing it to splinters in a matter of seconds. "You two coming?" he called over his shoulder.

Floor by floor, Resus cut his way through the doors leading to the dormitories, revealing dozens of still-sleeping children in each room. One by one they began to scream, the terrible sound growing louder and louder until it almost blocked out the noise of the chainsaw.

"I don't think the Nightwatchman approves of your DIY!" yelled Cleo.

"Wait till he sees this!" bellowed Resus as they reached the bottom of the staircase, and he thrust the whirring blade into the brickwork. The chainsaw sank through like a hot knife in butter.

Once he'd created a rectangle large enough to fit through, Resus kicked at the wall and watched in satisfaction as it crumbled. The trio stepped out into the warm jungle air. "There's very little in life that can't be solved by ripping it to bits with a chainsaw!" grinned Resus before slipping it back under his cape.

Ursula ran over to them. "You did it!" she cried. "You saved your friend!"

"We've got Spider to thank for that," said Luke. "Is he awake yet?"

"He's looking after Morag," Ursula said. "She's suddenly fallen ill."

Luke smiled thoughtfully. "And I think I know why…" he said. "Follow me." He led the way through the bushes and back into the clearing, and hurried past the group of astonished children to stand by the second witch. Morag lay on the ground, clutching at her stomach.

"Did you ever wonder why the Nightwatchman was able to follow you, no matter how far you travelled each night?" Luke asked Ryan, who had jumped up to join them. "Why the tower was always just the other side of the trees?"

"It's weird," replied the ghost. "I suppose he

could have been watching us."

"He *was* watching you," Luke agreed. "From right here within the camp – night after night, day after day." He pointed at Morag. "All thanks to her."

"What do you mean?" asked Resus.

Luke turned to the young troll sitting with the other children by the fire. "Jorden, isn't it? Would you come here a second…?"

Nervously, the troll crossed over to join the trio. "Look at Morag," Luke instructed. "Tell me what you see."

Jorden swallowed hard. "It… It's just Morag," he said. "She's a witch. She, er … leads us through the jungle at night. And she's very pretty."

"Exactly," said Luke. "She's very pretty – and that was nearly enough to fool me, too. When Spider first brought us here, I couldn't take my eyes off Ursula – but I barely gave Morag a second glance. *She's not under an enchantment charm!*"

"He's right!" gasped Resus. "I can turn away from her without feeling like I have to look back. She's not a witch at all!"

Morag suddenly jumped to her feet. "Oh, you're so clever, wolf-boy!" she shrieked. "But

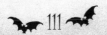 111

you'll never beat us! You'll never beat *him*!" In a flash, she transformed into a raven and flew at Luke's face, claws extended.

"Spider!" Luke cried.

"Power of a sabre hawk!" yelled the ogre. Then he screeched his unearthly cry at Morag's raven. The children clapped their hands to their ears as the sound echoed around the clearing. The bird fell to the ground, stunned, and changed straight back into human form, where once again she lay, trembling.

"Morag's been leading you in circles," Luke said to Ursula. "That's why you've never been able to find the Hex Hatches to let you take the children home. But you already knew that, didn't you?"

"I suspected you'd be the one to work it out," said Ursula with a smile.

"It took me a while," Luke admitted. "But I finally realized that if children's terror was feeding the Nightwatchman, only children's laughter could defeat him."

"And it's more powerful than any spell I can conjure up," smiled the witch. "I had a feeling... But all I could do was keep Morag busy until someone arrived who could really save the Nightwatchman's victims."

Morag sneered at Ursula, then clutched at her stomach again.

"She's ill," said Cleo.

Luke nodded. "And I know the best medicine."

Chapter Eleven
The Laughter

"Tell me why we're doing this again?"

asked Cleo as Luke daubed her bandages with face paint that Resus had found in his cloak.

"We're trying to recreate my dream," Luke said patiently.

Cleo's brow furrowed. "What? The one where you had to fight your mum?"

"No," said Luke, painting on a red nose. "The one I was having when Kian came to tell me you were missing – about the circus."

"I thought your dream circus had performing animals in it?"

"We've got Spider," said Luke. "He can be any animal we want. The rest of it is up to us." He held a mirror in front of Cleo's face and smiled. "There!"

"Why do *I* have to be the clown?" she complained.

"Because Resus is doing acrobatics and Ursula will be performing magic tricks," answered Luke.

"What about you?" asked Cleo. "What's your job?"

"Keeping an eye on the tower," said Luke. "My laughter up on the rooftop really hurt the Nightwatchman – that's why he came flapping into my nightmare, because I'd made you and Resus smile. Now we just have to make the others laugh too."

Cleo pulled on the brightly coloured baggy trousers Resus had found inside his cape and fastened the braces. "How will we do that?" she asked. "How can we get inside their heads if we aren't asleep alongside them like you were with me?"

Luke pointed to Morag, who lay paralysed by the containment spell Ursula had cast over her. Her eyes were locked open and staring. "We've got a direct line to the Nightwatchman himself."

"OK," said Cleo, finally convinced. "Let's go!"

Luke squeezed her hand, then jogged out into the jungle clearing. The rescued children were sitting in rows, waiting excitedly for the show to begin.

"Ladles and jelly spoons!" Luke announced. "Welcome to the funniest circus in the world!" Ursula clicked her fingers and fireworks erupted in the sky above them. The children watched in awe.

Morag could do nothing more than let out a strangulated *eep!*, her mouth held rigid by the spell.

When the fireworks had ended, Luke announced: "Please welcome the Incredible Negative!"

To great applause, Resus swung down from a nearby tree on a length of vine. He scooped up three large, round peaches from the ground and began to juggle, taking a bite from each as they passed his mouth until nothing was left but the hard pits in the centre. Then, finally, he popped them into his mouth and spat them out at Cleo, who was sitting near by.

Cleo wobbled into the makeshift circus ring and chased after Resus, tripping, falling and somersaulting as she went. The children clapped their hands and laughed gleefully at the clown.

A roar echoed across the clearing. Luke looked up to see the Nightwatchman on top of the tower, writhing around in anguish. For a brief moment, the children's laughter faltered.

"Keep going!" Luke urged. Resus winked at the audience and raced for the tree again, Cleo in hot pursuit. Digging his fake vampire nails into the bark, Resus deftly climbed out of Cleo's path and she smacked comically into the thick trunk. The audience burst into laughter, and this time giggles could be heard from inside the tower as well.

"It's working!" Luke hissed to his friends.

"Morag is transmitting everything we do directly into the dreams of the kids in the tower!"

Keeping up the pretence of being angry, Cleo folded her arms grumpily and went to sit down. Resus quickly unclipped his false fangs and tossed them onto the ground where she was about to sit. She yelped in pain as they bit into her bottom and jumped up, running in circles. The children laughed even louder.

"STOP IT!" screamed an agonized voice. The Nightwatchman was clearly in pain.

"OK, Ursula – you're next!"

The beautiful witch took to the stage and produced a bouquet of flowers for Cleo's clown, who made her exit. Next Ursula clicked her fingers and six pure white doves appeared in the air above her.

Morag's eyes were now wide with terror, and up on the tower the Nightwatchman was screaming and clutching at his pounding head.

Cleo joined Luke at the edge of the clearing. "Well?" she asked.

Luke grinned. "It's only a matter of time now," he said. "Just look at their happy faces – and listen to those laughs coming from the tower.

Nothing can go wrong!"

He had barely finished speaking when a ragged, dirty figure staggered into the circus ring, his clothes torn and his face scratched, clutching a small vial of blood.

It was Sir Otto Sneer.

"Another clown!" shouted Addie in excitement.

"I've walked for hours," wheezed Scream Street's landlord, barely able to stand. "And I can't find that blasted Hex Hatch anywhere!" The audience, thinking this was part of the act, laughed and pointed.

"Be quiet, you freaks!" roared Sir Otto.

"No, it is *you* who should be silent," commanded Ursula, pointing a trembling finger at the landlord. "Or I shall reveal your terrible secret!"

Sir Otto was taken aback. His cheeks paled and he began absentmindedly to stroke the white silk scarf around his neck. "Terrible ... secret...?" he breathed hoarsely.

"What's up with him?" hissed Resus.

Luke shrugged. "I dunno, but he looks as though he's going to faint!"

The landlord clamped his teeth down on his cigar and struggled to regain his composure.

"You're talking nonsense, you stupid woman!" he said quickly. Snatching a magic wand from Ursula's pile of props and holding the sparkling star over his head, he bellowed, "I know what to do. I'll magic myself back home!"

"I wouldn't do that if I were you…" began Luke, but it was too late. Sir Otto Sneer had cast the only spell inside the wand – and was starting to shrink.

"What's going on?" he squeaked. "What have you done?"

The effect was instant. The children in the audience roared with laughter, and from the doorway Resus had cut in the side of the tower, the zombie stumbled out, tears of mirth running down his green, decaying face.

"That's the kid you untied!" exclaimed Cleo.

Luke nodded. "And hopefully he will have helped someone else out of their bed…" Just then, another child emerged from the tower – a skeleton this time, also giggling. Other children streamed out into the daylight after them, all still laughing at the wonderful dream they'd just woken from.

At the top of the now deserted tower, the Nightwatchman howled out a final, agonized

scream. Then he and the tower both exploded
into clouds of whispery shadow, which quickly

evaporated in the bright sunlight.

"It worked!" cried Cleo. The tower, the Nightwatchman – and even Morag – had gone.

"Never mind that!" shrieked a tiny voice. "Somebody help me!"

Spider bent down to scoop up Sir Otto. "I thinks I'd better gives this little cherub to you," he said, handing the squirming figure to Resus.

The vampire took hold of the miniature landlord and peered down at him. "Oh my, Grandma," he teased. "What a tiny, little everything you've got!" Sir Otto was still shouting insults as Resus tucked him away inside his cape.

Luke picked up the vial of witch's blood from where Sir Otto had dropped it and stared into its sparkling contents. "Well, that was a stroke of luck," he grinned. "Now we just have to hope that giving this back to Ursula will work."

"I doubt it," said the witch, coming over to join them. "It's not my blood, is it?"

Luke looked horrified. "But … but you said you had the same blood in your veins as your mum…"

Ursula shrugged, but there was a twinkle in her eye. "It's more or less the same – but if you

want to be sure that returning the relic will have the desired effect, there's really only one person you should be talking to…"

The witch reached up and pulled a single hair from her head. Muttering a spell under her breath, she tossed the hair into the campfire. The flames erupted, giving off a shower of blue sparks and causing Luke, Resus and Cleo to shield their eyes. When they looked back, a figure was standing in the blaze.

"Nelly Twist!" gasped Cleo.

"The very same," smiled the older witch. "And it's good to see you all again. But seeing as contacting me in this way goes against all the rules, I assume my daughter must have a very good reason for summoning me here…"

Luke held out the vial of blood. "We have to return this to you," he said. "It served its purpose, but now it will do more good if you would take it back."

Nelly Twist paused to consider this. "If you're sure," she said after a while, "so be it." She took the bottle from Luke and blew a kiss to her daughter. Then, in a roar of fire, both she and the vial vanished.

Luke smiled. Although they couldn't see it, he was confident that the blue section of the doorway in Scream Street had just disappeared in a shower of sparks, as the red part had done when they'd returned the vampire's fang.

"Now," said Ursula, "I've got a lot of children

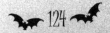

to return to their homes – with Spider's help, of course."

"When we get back to Scream Street, I'll ask Zeal Chillchase to open some official Hex Hatches for you," said Luke. "They're much easier to find and everyone will be home before they know it."

Ursula hugged Luke tightly and planted a kiss on his cheek. "Thank you!" she beamed. "As soon as you arrived I had a feeling you'd be the one to help." Luke blushed as Resus pulled a sickly kissy face over the witch's shoulder.

As Ursula hurried away to spread the news, Cleo turned to her friends. "Well, I suppose I should thank you two bumblers for rescuing me!"

"And every other kid in that tower," added Resus.

"Yeah, I guess…" Cleo grinned. "So, what do you think? Should we return the next relic? The mummy's heart?"

"Could be quite an adventure," said Resus.

Luke put an arm around each of his friends and smiled. "Go on, then," he said. "If it turns out anything like this one, it should be a bit of a laugh!"

Tommy Donbavand was born and brought up in Liverpool and has worked at numerous careers that have included clown, actor, theatre producer, children's entertainer, drama teacher, storyteller and writer. His non-fiction books for children and their parents, *Boredom Busters* and *Quick Fixes for Bored Kids*, have helped him to become a regular guest on radio stations around the UK and he also writes for a number of magazines, including *Creative Steps* and Scholastic's *Junior Education*.

Tommy sees his comedy-horror series *Scream Street* as what might have resulted had Stephen King been the author of *Scooby Doo*. "Writing *Scream Street* is fangtastic fun," he says. "I just have to be careful not to scare myself too much!" Tommy had so much fun writing the first Scream Street books that he decided to set Luke, Resus and Cleo another quest so he'd have an excuse to write some more.

You can find out more about Tommy and his books at his website: www.tommydonbavand.com